When You're a Pirate Dog

and Other Pirate Poems

When You're a Pirate Dog

and Other Pirate Poems

Eric Ode   Jim Harris

PELICAN PUBLISHING COMPANY

Gretna 2012

To Kim, my favorite explorer, with love.—Eric

To Heather Vanessa, a swashbuckling pirate at heart, who helped me so much in gathering references, making costumes, and critiquing. And who makes the best cinnamon rolls this side of heaven.—Jim

The word "Pelican" and the depiction of a pelican are trademarks of Pelican Publishing Company, Inc., and are registered in the U.S. Patent and Trademark Office.

ISBN 9781455614936
e-book ISBN 9781455614943

Printed in Singapore
Published by Pelican Publishing Company, Inc.
1000 Burmaster Street, Gretna, Louisiana 70053

When You're a Pirate Dog

When you're a pirate dog,
the pirates treat you well.
And no one minds your doggy breath
or hates your doggy smell.
And no one worries if you shed
or where you lay your shaggy head,
and all the fleas are theirs instead
when you're a pirate dog.

When you're a pirate dog,
they pet you when they're able.
They never mind their manners
as they feed you from the table.
And when they sing a pirate song
in jolly voices, loud and strong,
you raise your chin and sing along
when you're a pirate dog.

When you're a pirate dog,
your life is free from troubles.
They never put you in a tub
with smelly soap and bubbles.
You spend your days on sea and sand
exploring with your pirate band,
and life is sweet and rather grand
when you're a pirate dog.

The Missing Pirate Flag

When sailing on the salty seas,
the bravest sailor's blood will freeze
if he should see that eerie sight,
a ghostly flag of black and white.

As evil pirates, each of us,
we pillage, plunder, cheat, and cuss.
From coast to coast, we boast and brag
and proudly fly our pirate flag.

But now our days are sad and bleak.
We lost our flag the other week.
We searched the ship with great concern,
from deck to hull and bow to stern.

We went below and checked the freight
from every keg to every crate,
but though we scrounged and looked around,
our pirate flag could not be found.

And so at last we had to choose
and find a flag that we could use.
But no one's frightened by this pair
of polka-dotted underwear.

I'm Kraken

I'm Kraken, the beast of the seas.
I gobble down sailors with ease.
It's true I'm a brute,
but you are so cute;
I'd sure like to give you a squeeze.

The Pirate and The Princess

A cold-hearted pirate was walking alone
and passed by a castle of cinder and stone.
He glanced at a tower and found as he neared
the face of a beautiful princess appeared.

She stood at her window. "Come save me," she wailed.
"A wicked old witch has me captured and jailed."
The buccaneer grunted and sighed, "What a hassle,"
then, grumbling, searched for a path to the castle.

He fought through a forest of thorn-covered trees
and flesh-eating ivy that chewed on his knees.
He swam through a moat and fought fierce, fishy creatures
and slime-covered serpents with frightening features.

He battled a dragon that guarded the tower,
whose blood-thirsty breathing smelled rancid and sour.
Then, reaching the tower, he broke down the door
and trudged up the steps to the twenty-third floor.

The princess embraced him. "My hero!" she cried.
"Now you'll be my husband, and I'll be your bride.
But first," she continued, "before we are married,
those clothes are atrocious. We're having them buried.

"And as for your beard, well, it simply must go.
My father, the king, wouldn't like it, you know.
And here is some perfume and sweet-smelling soap.
You don't mean to smell so disgusting, I hope.

"You'll learn about culture and royal finances.
You'll drink tea at ten and attend fancy dances.
And dozens of servants will be at your bidding."
The buccaneer shuddered. "You've got to be kidding!

"I gather, young lady, you think I'd desire it.
You can't make a gentleman out of a pirate."
He turned for the door, and he said with a wince,
"The next time you're captured, please wait for a prince."

Captain Myrtle's Turtle Boots

Pirate Captain Myrtle caught two turtles by the stream.
"A perfect pair!" she shouted. "They're like something from a dream.
I'll take them into town to make a brand new pair of boots.
These two are worn and tattered. I'm in need of substitutes."

So Myrtle took the turtles to the boot and buckle shop.
The owner looked them over from the bottom to the top.
"They're mighty nice." He whistled as he tapped one on the shell.
"I ain't made turtle boots before. I hope they turn out well."

He measured Myrtle's ankles, and he measured Myrtle's toes.
He scratched his chin. "I'll have them done by Friday, I suppose."
Then Captain Myrtle thanked the man, and he smiled back at Myrtle
and set about to build her boots entirely of turtle.

Those boots were like no others in their color and design.
On Friday, Myrtle slipped them on, and, oh, they fit her fine!
But turtles travel slowly. It's a fact you've heard before.
So forty minutes later, she was nearly out the door.

When Stan Was a Student

When Stan was a student
in pirating class,
he'd never be cranky.
He'd never be crass.
While others were wicked
and reckless and wild,
he sat prim and proper.
He studied and smiled.

His teacher said Stanley
was sweet and polite.
You'd never see Stanley
get into a fight.
He'd try to be thoughtful.
He'd follow each rule.
So, needless to tell you,
he flunked out of school.

Treasure Hunt

We're Captain Casper's mighty crew.
We're merciless and bold.
We're on this island deep at sea
to claim our buried gold.
We set out seven years ago,
our treasure chest in hand,
and came to this forsaken place
of barnacles and sand.

We dug a hole. We dug it deep,
where no one might suspect,
and lowered down the treasure chest
we'd come back to collect.
Then Casper said to fill the hole.
It took us quite awhile.
And then he said to draw a map
of this deserted isle.

We drew the hills. We drew the trees,
the rivers, and the bay.
We drew the shells and rocks and twigs,
and then we sailed away.
Yes, that was seven years ago,
but now we have returned.
We've yet to find that treasure chest.
We're getting quite concerned.

We've dug about a hundred holes.
We've searched from here to there.
The captain's face is lobster-red.
He's pulling out his hair.
He says he'll have us walk the plank.
He says he'll have our necks.
It's true we made a dandy map.
We just forgot the X.

A Few Really Bad Pirate Jokes

Q: When pirate MaryAnn McCall
       was clobbered by a cannonball,
       why did it never harm her?
A: She wore a suit of arrrr-mor.

Q: What's the favorite vegetable
       of hungry pirate folks?
A: Arrrr-tichokes.

Q: What does pirate Green,
       who's big and tough and mean,
       use to make a pillow?
A: An arrrr-madillo

Pirate Pat's Fancy Hat

Vile and vicious Pirate Pat
adores his fancy pirate hat.
Its shiny band of finest leather
holds a long and lacy feather.
Follow Pat and you will find
that frilly feather floats behind,
and as it bumps your nose and chin,
you'll smirk a bit. And then you'll grin.
You'll snicker, chortle, smile, and chuckle,
giggle till your ankles buckle,
laugh so hard your sides will ache!
But that will be a big mistake.
Vile and vicious Pirate Pat
will think it's *him* you're laughing at,
or, even worse, his fancy hat.
And, bet your life,
he won't like that!

Red Eye Jack, the Pirate Ghost

A pirate ghost came through my door
and shouted with a salty roar,
"Avast, ye swine! I'm Red Eye Jack.
My blood is cold. My heart is black.
I live in places dark and dank
and laugh as others walk the plank.
Some men are tough, but I'm the most,"
said Red Eye Jack, the pirate ghost.

"I'm here to take you as my crew.
We'll do the things that pirates do.
We'll pilfer, swindle, lie, and curse.
When things are bad, we'll make them worse.
We'll fight with swords and guns and whips.
We'll battle merchant sailing ships.
We'll raid and loot and brag and boast,"
said Red Eye Jack, the pirate ghost.

"We'll live our lives upon the waves,
exploring dark and deadly caves
with secret rooms and hidden traps
and walls of ancient treasure maps.
Now off we go to cheat and steal.
You hoist the sails. I'll take the wheel.
We'll plunder towns along the coast,"
said Red Eye Jack, the pirate ghost.

"It's kind of you to ask," I said,
"but Mother says it's time for bed.
You're welcome to the upper bunk.
An extra pillow's in the trunk."
He sniffed and sighed, then up he crawled.
"There's eggs and tea at ten," I called.
"I'm rather fond of buttered toast,"
said Red Eye Jack, the pirate ghost.

Pirate Stew

When told to feed a pirate crew,
a pot of pirate stew will do.
You'll need a kettle, big and rusty,
thick with grime and rather dusty.
Add a dozen buzzard eggs;
sixty-seven spider legs;
thick, congealing spotted eel;
piles of spoiled banana peel;
a cold and moldy minnow spleen;
a lizard gizzard, slimy green.
Now add some musty camel meat
and rancid ants with fuzzy feet.
Then stir it up. (Excuse the smell.)
No other food will feed as well.
The crew will cheer to see it's true;
You've made a pot of pirate stew!
They'll call the meal a splendid feast.
They'll eat a dozen bowls at least!
But should they say you ought to try it,
tell them, "No! I'm on a diet."

Biscuits

"You best beware the biscuits, men,"
the cook called from the galley door.
"They're tougher than they should have been.
I dropped one, and it cracked the floor."

A pirate picked a biscuit up
and muttered as he gave a gnaw,
"I'd sooner eat my coffee cup.
I'm pretty sure I broke my jaw."

But Captain Jake, he opened wide.
He bit a biscuit hard and deep.
And every man was horrified
as Captain Jake began to weep.

He gave a sniff and wiped an eye.
"I'm sorry boys," said Captain Jake.
"I reckon I've a right to cry.
They're just like Mamma used to make."

Sing Hey Hi-Dee Ho!

Sing hey hi-dee ho!
Give a holler or two.
We're three mighty pirates—
a frightening crew.
And stories are told
of the things that we do.
Sing hey hi-dee ho!
Give a holler or two.

Sing hey hi-dee ho!
There's a song in our heart.
We're fearless and famous.
We're never apart.
We don't have a boat
so we ride in a cart.
Sing hey hi-dee ho!
There's a song in our heart.

Sing hey hi-dee ho!
Give a shout and a yell!
Our mule pulls the cart.
He's our captain as well.
He's really quite fine
if you don't mind the smell.
Sing hey hi-dee ho!
Give a shout and a yell!

So let the sky thunder,
and let the wind blow.
We'll face any danger
wherever we go.
And songs will be sung,
and the people will know
we're three mighty pirates.
Sing hey hi-dee ho!

Even as James Jenkins, the navigator, stares at his new compass, he has a feeling that the ship is going in circles.

Sam keeps a weather eye out for whales, other ships, and the pizza delivery guy.

Pirates love games of chance. Go Fish is their favorite.

Bang, bang, OUCH! Bang, bang, OUCH! The carpenters on the *Puffer Fish* aren't very good with hammers.

With only one toilet on the *Puffer Fish,* tempers flare when Roger finds an interesting article in a *National Geographic* magazine.

The Puf

er Fish

Pirate Manual

Greasy, the ship's cook, serves turtle soup every day because he doesn't like fast food.

Captain Bob built an extra-low crow's nest for crew members who are afraid of heights.

The pirate's manual states:
1. Place prisoner on a plank of wood extending from the side of the ship.
2. Have the prisoner walk to the end of the plank.
Fortunately for prisoner J. J. Jackson, the page with step 3 is missing.

Ned is called an old sea dog partly because of his years of experience but mostly because he has fleas.

Pirates use cannonballs for bowling.

Tourist class

Due to poor math skills, first mate Snerd Peabody miscalculates and overfills the longboat, sending the captain's treasure to Davy Jones' locker. Followed shortly by Snerd Peabody.

The smell is so terrible that even the pigs hold their noses when the pirates are close by.

No One Tells the Captain

No one tells the captain
his haircut is a mess.
No one tells the captain
he cheats when playing chess.
No one tells the captain
his jokes aren't very funny.
No one tells the captain
his nose is red and runny.

No one tells the captain
he's singing out of key,
or tells him he's to blame
when we're lost again at sea.
No one tells the captain
he's cranky and he's rude,
his manners are atrocious,
and his beard is full of food.

His jacket may be moldy.
His hat may look absurd.
And maybe he has awful breath,
but no one says a word.
It's true he needs a bar of soap,
a toothbrush, and a comb.
But no one tells the captain,
or they'll be swimming home.

Jerry, the Juggling Pirate

He's Jerry, the juggling pirate.
He's seven feet tall at the shoulders.
He juggles with ease anything that he pleases—
cannonballs, barrels, and boulders.

Donkeys and monkeys and anchors and chains
and seventeen swords in a sack.
A staggering sight as they loop left and right
and soar from his front to his back.

He's Jerry, the juggling pirate.
He's daring and dashing and clever.
But ask, "Do you miss?" and he'll shrug and say this,
"Well, sometimes, but practically never."

And then he'll begin with a toss and a spin.
Such skill! You can't help but admire it.
You'll holler! You'll cheer! But you won't stand too near
to Jerry, the juggling pirate.

Crusty and Rusty and Musty McGee

Crusty and Rusty and Musty McGee,
the three fiercest pirates to travel the sea,
were sailing their ship through an uncharted ocean
when suddenly came a fantastic commotion.

The waves began swelling. The sea began churning.
The ship started rocking and tossing and turning.
Then, up from the waters, a creature arose
with claws on his flippers and spikes on his nose.

His eyes were like fire. His teeth were like nails.
His body was covered in silvery scales.
He circled the ship, and he chuckled with glee
at Crusty and Rusty and Musty McGee.

"It looks like I've found me a marvelous feast.
I'll eat you at once," said that hideous beast.
"You don't frighten me," Crusty said with a yawn.
Then, chomp, went the serpent, and Crusty was gone.

Then Rusty stepped up with a tip of his hat.
"You'll find," said the pirate, "I'm stronger than that."
The creature said, "Yes, I imagine that's true."
Then, munch, went the beast, and he ate Rusty, too.

Then Musty stepped forward and said, "That's enough.
I'm stronger than strong, and I'm tougher than tough.
You don't stand a chance with a pirate like me.
I'm fierce and I'm fearless," said Musty McGee.

That sea monster grimaced. He looked rather ill.
He said, "My dear fellow, I've eaten my fill.
You chaps are a gristly, bristly bunch.
I'll never again eat a pirate for lunch."

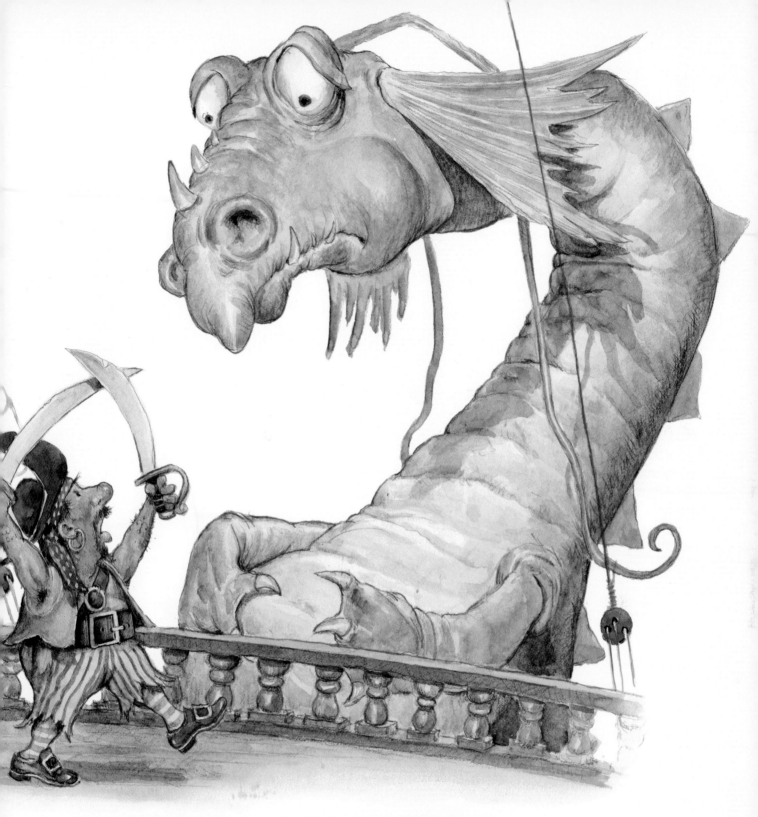

"I knew you'd be frightened," the pirate declared.
"You look mighty strong, but you're timid and scared."
He laughed at the beast. "You're a cowardly soul."
The beast sighed at Musty and swallowed him whole.

And this ends our tale. You might find it offending.
It's likely you'd hoped for a happier ending.
Perhaps, my dear friend, you'll be happy to hear
that sea monster's tummy-ache lasted a year.

The Pirate Molly Mae

The sailors tell the stories of the pirate Molly Mae,
who rode a barracuda out of Turtle Bottom Bay.
She wrestled a volcano off of Nikki Wikki Isle
and kept a pair of pythons and a cranky crocodile.

They say she fought a tiger shark and kissed a polar bear.
They say she met a tidal wave and froze it with a stare.
I've heard it said she makes her bed from oyster shells and stones.
They say the sea is in her blood and sand is in her bones.

The day when I met Molly, she was battling at sea,
and cannons shook the morning as she sipped a cup of tea.
The cannonballs were flying. They were bursting left and right.
And Molly caught one in her fist, and then she took a bite.

She chewed and chewed that cannonball as if she had a plan.
Then, all at once, she spat it out—an iron frying pan.
And as explosions shook the ship around our feet and legs,
she fried us up some sausages and half a dozen eggs.

Missing

Attention Crew:

If you should see or hear about
a creature with a slimy snout
and yellow gills and purple scales
and feathers on its seven tails,
a creature fat and foul and smelly
creeping on its bulging belly,
tell me quickly. Thanks a bunch.
Until it's caught, I can't make lunch.
- The Cook

Marooned on Coconut Island

There's coconut sandwiches,
coconut steaks,
coconut puddings
and coconut cakes.
Coconut fritters
and coconut hams,
coconut jellies
and coconut jams.

Coconut sherbet
and coconut custard,
coconut sausage
with coconut mustard.
Coconut gravy
on coconut roast
and coconut butter
on coconut toast.

I've been on this island
for seventeen years
with mountains of coconuts
up to my ears.
My stomach's a wreck,
and my brain is like putty.
Rescue me quick
or I'll go coco-nutty!

A Sea Serpent's Life

A sea serpent's life is a lonely existence,
a story of loss and rejection.
When sailors have spotted me off in the distance,
they sail in the other direction.

It could be my manners they find unappealing.
It could be the way that I greet them.
It could be my temper, but I've got a feeling
it's mostly the fact that I eat them.

Captain Keel's Fishing Trip

"Someone take my captain hat,
and someone take the wheel.
Today I'm going fishing,"
shouted pirate Captain Keel.
"I'm off to catch the biggest fish
the world has ever seen;
a fish as big as twenty sharks
and every bit as mean."

He grabbed a long and rusty chain,
an anchor for a hook,
then baited it with seven hams
he borrowed from the cook.
And then the captain took a seat
and waited for a bite.
He felt a nibble, then a tug,
and bravely held on tight.

He braced his boots against the deck.
His eyes were proud and stern
as all about the pirate ship
the waves began to churn.
Then from the sea the creature leapt,
a fierce and scaly beast;
a fish as wide as any ship
and twice as long, at least.

But as it circled through the air,
the pirates gave a shout
to see that creature give a wink
and spit the anchor out.
"You've lost him," cried the
    second mate.
"That fish is far too strong."
The captain threw the chain aside
and said, "That's where you're wrong."

He grit his teeth and waited
as the sea grew inky black.
Then, as the creature rose again,
he jumped upon its back.
The creature tumbled,
    tossed, and turned,
but Keel would not let go.
Then, all at once, they vanished
as the monster dove below.

"A dreadful shame," the
    cook declared.
"Let's bow our heads and kneel.
Today we lost a fearless friend,
the mighty Captain Keel."
A day went by. A week. A month.
Till one day, deep at sea,
they found the captain at the wheel,
alive as he could be.

"A miracle!" the crew declared.
"We thought you must be dead."
"But what about the fish?"
    they asked.
The captain shook his head.
"I had to let him go," he said.
"He wasn't worth the bother.
Tomorrow, when I try again,
I hope to catch his father."

The Pirate's Birthday Party

At the pirate's birthday party
there are streamers and balloons.
The guests are wearing party hats
and singing birthday tunes.
They're playing Toss the Cannonball
and Pirate Hide and Seek
and games of Pin the Cracker
to the Purple Parrot's Beak.

The birthday guest of honor
has the special birthday chair.
His clothes are almost kind of clean.
He even combed his hair.
He's blowing out the candles
as he makes his birthday wish
on squid and seaweed birthday cake
with frosting made of fish.

A Tight Fit

Me elbow's stuck inside me ear.
An anchor's up against me rear.
A parrot's pressed against me cheeks.
I haven't seen the sea in weeks.

Me nose is flat. Me arm is numb.
The cabin boy is on me thumb.
The captain's toes are in me beard.
Me wooden leg has disappeared.

It's true a pirate's life is hard.
Me face is squished. I'm scratched and scarred.
Before we take another trip,
I hope we get a bigger ship.

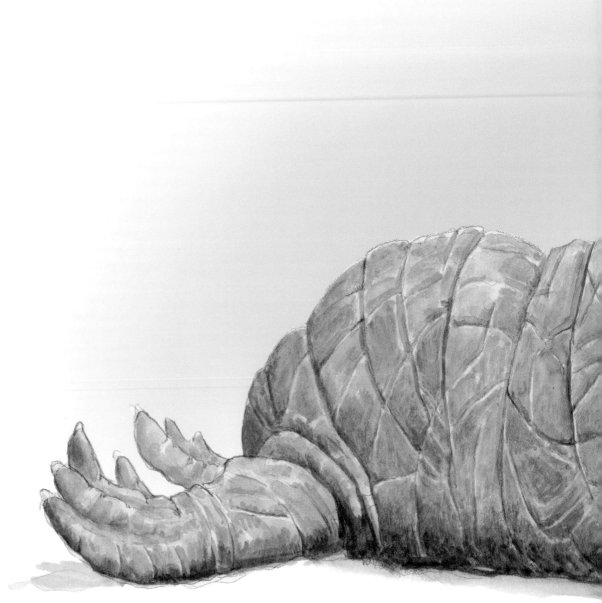

A Pirate's Curse

I once was a pirate,
a bold buccaneer;
the kind that the bravest
of sailors would fear.
I charted my courses
for various treasures.
I looted and pillaged
for profits and pleasures.

But once, on an island,
remote and forsaken,
I found me a treasure
I should not have taken.
A witch owned this treasure.
She guarded it well,
protecting that gold
with a magical spell.

I grabbed it, and soon
I was fat as a whale.
My arms became flippers.
I sprouted a tail.
My nose became swollen
with whiskers beneath,
and two yellow tusks
sprouted out from my teeth.

So now I'm a walrus
because of a curse.
It may seem outrageous,
but things could be worse.
I'm smelly and wrinkled
and couldn't be wetter,
but most folks will tell you
I've never looked better.

Commodore Quail

I'm one nasty pirate; I'm Commodore Quail.
And Pineapple Pond is the ocean I sail.
Let others be bankers and bakers and tailors.
I'm living my life as the bravest of sailors.

This ship has been with me through trials and perils.
I built her myself out of boxes and barrels.
She's riddled with termites and leaking, I think.
But this pond's so small, we can't possibly sink.

I've been on these waters ten years and a day,
and no other pirate dares get in my way.
I'm ruthless and toothless and tough as a nail.
I'm one nasty pirate. I'm Commodore Quail!

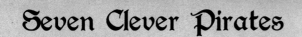

Seven Clever Pirates

We're seven clever pirates.
We're confident and wise
with wooden pegs instead of legs
and patches on our eyes.
We cast our sails and set a course
for where adventure lies.
It's no surprise. We're seven clever pirates.

We're seven clever pirates.
We're doing as we please.
We're impolite. We fuss and fight
and rule the seven seas.
We check our maps and watch the stars
and travel with the breeze.
A life of ease for seven clever pirates.

We're seven clever pirates.
We're sailors with a plan.
We left the shore a month or more
to travel where we can.
But no one raised the anchor,
so we're still where we began,
a mighty clan of seven clever pirates.

Off the Map

"Batten down the hatches, boys," said Captain Jasper Jones.
"There's something waiting just ahead. I feel it in me bones.
Now what it be, I can not say," he told his fearless crew.
"But this is why we're pirates, men, and this is what we do.

"We've sailed ourselves right off the map to somewhere never seen.
Perhaps we'll find uncharted places, tropical and green.
Perhaps a mighty ocean beast will lead us to a trap.
But no one knows what waits beyond the edges of the map.

"So keep a weather eye, me lads, and best ye say a prayer.
Win or fail, we're setting sail where others never dare."
"Hooray, hoorah!" The pirates cheered and shouted one by one.
They hoped the best and headed west into the setting sun.

And this is where we end the tale of Jasper and his crew
for no one's seen them since that day. This much we know is true.
Now some have guessed their days were blessed and others think them cursed.
And some believe the very best while some believe the worst.
But someone has to set the course, and someone must be first
to find the place where secrets and adventures overlap
and first to find what waits beyond the edges of the map.